Taffie & Trista
Learn Rhyme and Reason

Taffie & Trista
Learn Rhyme and Reason

by Krista Remias

TATE PUBLISHING & *Enterprises*

Published by Tate Publishing & Enterprises, LLC
127 E. Trade Center Terrace | Mustang, Oklahoma 73064 USA
1.888.361.9473 | www.tatepublishing.com

Tate Publishing is committed to excellence in the publishing industry. The company reflects the philosophy established by the founders, based on Psalm 68:11,
"The Lord gave the word and great was the company of those who published it."

Book design copyright © 2011 by Tate Publishing, LLC. All rights reserved.
Cover and interior design by Chris Webb
Illustrations by Mike Lee

Published in the United States of America

ISBN: 978-1-61739-932-9
1. Fiction / Christian / General
2. Fiction / Contemporary Women
11.04.25

Dedication

Dedicated to my dearest family and friends who love me enough to want more for me than I want for myself. You know who you are. Keep praying! You never know what adventure will be next!

To my precious BFF, Taffie, who believes in me when I can't even believe in myself. I love you.

But mostly all thanks and praise goes to my King. He is the love of my life and the Savior of my soul. All glory goes to him!

Taffie was a lovely red-headed child who lived in the small town of Grovetucky. She was the oldest girl of ten children. She and her five sisters and four brothers lived in a small house on the west side of town. She loved to play outside as she sang, danced, and skipped rope.

The children attended a private school taught by the finest scholars the little town had to offer. The teachers were strict in their discipline as well as in their lessons. Taffie had a hard time as she sat in the classroom. She loved to be outside in the sunshine. Many times she would find herself in the corner as her mind wandered to what she was going to do when she got out of school. Her report card usually had unsatisfactory marks in the "conduct" column. It wasn't that she was unruly, but that she had no interest in the things that the teachers had to offer.

Taffie and her family went to church every week. She loved see her friends and listen to music, but the droning of the elderly pastor always put her to sleep. She knew that she should stay awake to listen to the message, but she would much rather be outside with her friends.

At home, Taffie tried hard to obey her parents. She did her chores and listened as her parents taught her right from wrong. She understood that they loved her, but she liked to have fun more than she liked to be obedient. It was a continual problem for her and her parents. As much as they lectured her, Taffie wouldn't listen.

At night, when the younger kids were in their beds, Taffie would open her window and climb down the vines to the garden outside her bedroom. There she would meet her older brothers and his friends. They would climb into the older kid's cars and go to the quarry. The kids all liked Taffie and teased her about being a little kid. To entertain them, she sang and danced.

One day, an older boy approached Taffie and said, "Hi! You sing great! I play the drums. Can I play while you sing?"

Well, Taffie had never actually talked to any of the older boys because her brothers wouldn't let her. This time they weren't around, so Taffie agreed. "Okay. What's your name, and what do you want to sing?"

Taffie was used to singing the songs she heard at church, but the boy said, "Let me teach you some new songs," to which Taffie eagerly agreed.

As the summer went on, Taffie and her new friend, Johnny, learned lots of songs. Soon they were singing for their friends almost every night. They grew to love one another that summer and decided that they would like to be married.

The problem was that Taffie's parents didn't know that she was going out of her bedroom window and not returning until the early morning hours. When Taffie told them that they wanted to be married, they were surprised. She was young, but Taffie convinced them that she knew what she was doing.

Taffie and Johnny were married on a bright sunny day in June. They settled in and soon had a baby. On the surface life was good, but after a few years, Taffie grew bored. She longed for the days when she would climb out the window and sing and dance with her friends. She and Johnny hadn't sung together for years, and their friends never seemed to have time to go out on the town anymore.

Frustrated and wanting to rediscover her old life, Taffie left Johnny and started a new life in a small house in Grovetucky. She and her little daughter never did find the exciting life she was looking for, but after a year or so, they settled into life. One day, Taffie met a tall, handsome man named Slim, who loved to sing and play the guitar. Over the course of the next year, they fell in love and were married.

Slim came from a small family led by his mother, Elouise. Elouise was a hard worker who loved her family and friends. Mostly, though, Elouise loved Jesus. She continually prayed to him for her children. When Taffie married Slim, she included Taffie in her prayers. "Bless my children, Lord and bring them unto you," was the way she started her prayers each morning. When she was done, she would thank him and wipe the tears from her eyes as she whispered, "Amen." Rising from her arthritic knees, she would commence with her day.

On Mother's Day, Taffie and Slim surprised Elouise and joined her at church. On that day, both Taffie and Slim heard the call of God and went forward to accept Jesus into their hearts. Elouise looked at her children with tears streaming down her face. She closed her eyes and thanked God for hearing her prayers.

Taffie had no idea what that meant, but it seemed like the right thing to do, so she obeyed. That night, she had a strange dream. In the morning, she was still puzzled, so she went to Elouise to help her understand.

"Elouise, can you help me? Last night I had a dream, and I need to know what it meant." Elouise looked at Taffie and nodded her head. Taffie continued, "Slim and I were standing at the front of the church, when a man in a brilliant white robe took me by the hand. He walked with me to a throne. I couldn't see the man on the throne, but the one in the white robe introduced me to the man whom he called Father. What does that mean?"

Elouise smiled and nodded. "You are now a part of God's family, Taffie. You will find family among the people of the church. You will have new sisters and brothers. I think the one in the white robe is Jesus. He is your brother and your friend. You can talk to him about anything. The one on the throne is God. It's a bit complicated, but if you read your Bible, you'll come to understand. Does that help?"

Taffie looked at Elouise for a moment before she spoke. "Not really, but I have a new Bible. I'll read it this afternoon and try to talk to God. Do I just talk to him like I talk to you?"

Elouise nodded. "Yes, Taffie, just talk to him. He loves you."

When Taffie got home, she picked up the new Bible that she had been given. She curled up in her favorite chair and bowed her head. *God,* Taffie started quietly, *I don't understand any of this. I need your help. Elouise said that I could talk to you about anything. I have some things that I need to tell someone, but I am afraid that if they knew—if you knew—you wouldn't love me. Can I really trust you?* Taffie grew still. She opened her Bible. Her eyes fell on the page.

"I loved you so much that I sent Jesus to die on a cross so that if you believe in me, you will not die but have eternal life." Taffie read and re-read the words in front of her. How could it be? Someone had to die for her to live with God? No one had ever loved her that much. She flipped a few pages and read more.

"I showed my great love for you by sending Jesus to die for you while you were still a sinner." By now, Taffie could not put the book down. "You need to know that God causes everything to work together for the good of those that love God and are called according to his purpose for them."

Here Taffie stopped and spoke to God. *If you can make all of the dark places in my life good, then please show me. God, some of them are as black as night. I can't imagine that anything good could come from my sin, but if you say it is so, I will believe.*

. . . .

Several years passed as Taffie and Slim walked with God. They worshiped at a little church in Grovetucky and were happy as their families grew. One Thanksgiving weekend, a new woman walked into the church service. At the end of the service, the pastor asked if there were anyone in the audience who needed to meet Jesus. At the altar call, the stranger walked to the front of the church and knelt at the altar. She didn't understand, but she knew that there was something she was supposed to hear. She prayed for Jesus to meet her there. Just as he had met Taffie and Slim years earlier, he came to meet this woman.

As she cried, she had a vision that Jesus picked her up and carried her before a throne. She heard Jesus say, "Father, this is my sister, Trista. She has come today to meet with you. She's hurt, Father, and tired." He turned to Trista and continued, "This is my Father. He is the almighty God. You come here today because he sent me to die on the cross for you. Will you accept this gift? Will you love me? Will you trust me to take care of your needs?"

Trista looked at Jesus with a tearstained face. "Yes," she replied. With that, Trista fell into the arms of Jesus as he embraced her. She rested in his arms.

When the service was over, Taffie and Slim left without ever realizing the scene unfolding in front of them. Trista left the altar quietly and went home to see her husband, Guss.

"Trista, how was church today?"

Trista looked at him with wonder in her eyes. "Guss, I met Jesus today. Let me tell you about it!" Trista told Guss about the service and about how she had a vision.

Guss was not happy. "Trista, I know all about Jesus. If you want to follow him, that's okay with me, but I'm not interested."

Trista looked down with a sad heart. "I understand, Guss. I need to do this for myself, though."

. . . .

Just after Christmas, Taffie was approached by the leaders of the church, as they wanted someone to befriend Trista. Taffie refused gently. "I'm not good with words. Please find someone else to be her friend. I really don't have the time … " She broke off, not knowing what else to say. While she had been studying, reading, and praying for many years, she still had secrets that she wasn't ready to reveal to the other ladies of the church. If she was friends with one of them, then she was afraid that they wouldn't like her anymore.

Trista was never aware of the conversation between Taffie and the leaders of the church, but God was, and he had other plans. That morning as Taffie had her time with God, she was complaining. "God, I don't know why I have to lead this study. Just like Moses, I'm slow of speech. I'm not a good leader." As she argued, she knew that her argument wasn't going to work. "Okay, okay. If I have to lead, then you give me the words, because they aren't going to come from me!"

God spoke to her heart, "Okay, Taffie. Thanks for the advice. You sit there, and I will put the words in your mouth." The first night of the study came, and Trista arrived with her Bible and the study guide. Trista had met a few women over the few weeks she had been coming to church, but as she entered the hall, she suddenly was afraid. *What if they don't like me? What if I don't fit in? What if…* As her fear mounted, she remembered the verse she had read that morning from the book of Isaiah. "Don't be afraid, for I am with you. Don't be discouraged, for I am your God. I will strengthen you and help you. I will hold you up with my victorious right hand."

Repeating it under her breath, she pushed open the door to the room. There, Taffie was talking with some of her friends. They had met briefly at the Christmas party but never really spoke.

Taffie opened the study in prayer and then began to talk about what they had read. Trista had been reading her Bible every night and was eager to know more about God. She leaned forward as the women spoke. They all seemed to know so much about how God worked and what he was like.

As the women shared, Trista felt her heart sink. She would never be like these women.

Taffie's voice broke into Trista's thoughts. "We aren't perfect women. We are forgiven. Since we have been forgiven so much, we are to forgive equally."

Trista immediately spoke, "That's all well and good for you, Taffie, but someone hurt me when I was little, and I will never forgive him. God wouldn't expect it of me, and I wouldn't do it even if he asked."

The words fell like rocks in the small room. Taffie shook her head and looked at Trista. "Trista, I know that if God wants you to forgive this man, he will change your heart. If you would like, we can talk after the lesson tonight."

With those words, a friendship was started between Taffie and Trista. They talked every day. Taffie shared what she learned in her studies, and Trista shared about her life with Guss. The winter months sped by, and soon the trees and flowers of spring turned into the heat of summer.

During the summer months, Trista and Taffie met in a local park to do a one-on-one

Bible study. They met under a huge old oak tree by the gazebo in the middle of the park. Each Thursday night they spent two hours talking and laughing and crying as they became sisters in every sense of the word. Each evening after their study time, the women would bow their heads and pray to God for the needs of the other. As they finished, they would open their eyes to the most amazing sunsets imaginable.

"Oh, Taffie." Trista sighed. "Look at the beautiful clouds in the sky. Do you suppose God put them there just for us?"

Taffie nodded. "Yep. Just for us. Look at that dark cloud over there in the corner. Isn't it beautiful against the gold one right beside it? And look at the maroon one in the middle. Where do you think it came from? Isn't God wonderful to show us this beautiful show?" The women grew silent as they watched the majesty unfold.

That summer, the friends had been praying for many things. Elouise had been sick, and Taffie was praying for her healing. Guss

hadn't accepted Jesus into his heart, so Trista was praying for him. Most of all though, the friends were praying for Taffie's daughter and for the baby she was to have that fall. Taffie was especially excited, as it was her first grandchild. The baby's name was to be Hope.

On a beautiful September day, Hope was born. Taffie called Trista with the news. "Trista, she's here! Hope is here! She's just beautiful. Oh, Trista, I love her so much."

Trista made all of the appropriate noises as she congratulated Taffie. "Taffie," said Trista, "I can't come today, but I will see Hope soon. Talk to you later!"

The next time that Trista heard from Taffie, things weren't going so well. Hope had a heart condition, and the doctors weren't sure what to do.

"Trista, Hope has a bad heart. The doctors have taken her from us and are talking about surgery. I'm scared. Trista, what should I do?" Taffie cried as she spoke.

in heaven. God saw Taffie and the rest of the family as the doctors broke the news to them.

Taffie listened to the news as if she were in a fog. It couldn't be real. Hope was supposed to come home. Her dream of the night before flashed in her mind. She knew that Hope was with Jesus, but she didn't want her there. She wanted her back with them. The clouds that surrounded her grew dark as she sat in on a hard plastic chair in disbelief.

"God, why? Oh, God, I loved her. She was so tiny. Why did you take my Hope? Please! I needed her!" Taffie poured her heart out to God, not knowing whether or not he even heard her. Taffie had to talk to someone, so she called Trista.

Guss answered the phone and told Taffie that Trista wasn't home. He listened as Taffie told him the news. "I'm sorry, Taffie. That's terrible. I'll have Trista call you when she gets home. Trista was at Bible study with two other friends when Guss finally reached her to tell her the news. The girls immediately went to Taffie's house.

When Taffie opened the door, Trista took her into her arms, and both of the women wept. Taffie told them the story of Hope's life and death and showed them the pictures they had taken over the six weeks of her life. Trista watched Taffie as she spoke. She saw the pain written all over her face. When Taffie was out of words, Trista put her arm around her friend and pulled her close. "God is with you, Taffie. He has a plan and a hope." Trista reminded her of the words they had learned the summer before in the park.

Taffie shook her head. "No, Trista. There is no more Hope. God took her from me. All I feel now is alone and afraid. I can't see how any of this is going to be for good. I wish I could see the light, but all I can see is the dark clouds hanging over my head."

Trista hugged her again as she whispered, "I love you, Taffie. It'll be okay. I don't know how, but it'll all be okay."

The next few days were a flurry of details and planning an event that wasn't ever supposed to happen, in Trista's opinion. The day of the funeral arrived as Trista poured out her complaint to God. "I think this is the most awful thing that could ever happen. I can't understand why a baby dies when evil people live and prosper. I really could use an answer on this one, God. Taffie needs my help, and for once I don't have any words to say to her. A little help, please?" Trista listened, but didn't hear any words come back to her from heaven. She sighed. It was so hard to understand how to be a good friend as well as to say all the right words and do all the right things.

She walked into the church to find it full of well-wishers and family. Taffie stood at the head of the church with the rest of the family. The altar was full of flowers and tiny bears. There where the communion table usually sat was the tiny casket. As Trista waited in line, she spoke with those around her. Small talk seemed so useless, but it was something to keep her mind off what was to come. As she approached Taffie, she reached out to her friend. They walked to the casket together.

Hope lay in the casket perfect and still. She looked like a porcelain doll. Trista wiped away tears as Taffie spoke. "Trista, help me. I can't stand this. It hurts so much. I know that God…" Taffie closed her eyes and sobbed. Trista held her hand and tried to think of the words she could say, but there just weren't any words that could fix Taffie's broken heart.

Trista led Taffie to the pew and they say sat together. "How can I help, Taffie? Do you need food? Do you need me to clean your house? What can I do to help? Oh, Taffie, please don't cry." Trista wrapped her arms around Taffie as she cried.

Finally, Taffie quieted and spoke to Trista without looking at her. "Trista, I have never been in such a dark place. I can't see God. I can't see you. I can't see two inches in front of my face. It's as though I'm in the darkest cave. I want to die."

Trista picked up her hand as they both gazed at the casket. "I'm here, my precious friend. Close your eyes and rest."

The service seemed to last for hours, yet too soon they were at the cemetery as Hope's earthly body was placed in the grave. Taffie tried to remind herself that Hope wasn't gone; she was in the arms of Jesus. The thought brought a sort of comfort, but over the next few days, the dark clouds seemed to hover over Taffie and Slim. It was hard to sleep and hard to concentrate on even the simplest of tasks. Taffie and Trista spoke every day. They cried together and spoke of trivial things. It was a difficult winter, but one day as the winter turned to spring, Taffie spoke to Trista of how she was healing.

"It isn't so bad anymore, Trista. I still wish that Hope was with us, but at least I can get out of the house and enjoy myself again. The days when the dark clouds come are further and further apart now. Thanks for being my friend."

Trista sighed. She hated that Taffie had to go through this and still didn't understand. She spoke with God about it on a regular basis, but she still didn't have a clear answer as to his plan. For now she just trusted that he was in charge, and she was glad that Taffie was ready to go back to being friends again.

The girls resumed praying together. One of the people they regularly prayed for was Trista's husband, Guss. He was a good man, but he hadn't ever accepted Jesus as his savior. Trista worried about it and talked about it to Taffie almost every time they got together. "What is keeping Guss from walking down that aisle, Taffie? Doesn't he see that I love Jesus, and he should too?"

Taffie nodded and prayed. She also prayed for Trista that she would learn to let God work things out. It was the lesson that she had learned from Hope's life. Sometimes she just had to let God work and trust that he had a plan.

That winter, Guss told Trista that he was ready to give his life to Jesus. In early spring he was baptized at the church where Trista had come to know her Savior. As they stood at the back of the church to be greeted by the congregation, every woman who had been in Bible study with Trista greeted Guss with the words, "We've been praying for you."

Guss looked at Trista with a raised eyebrow and said, "Is that all you and your friends do is pray for your husbands?"

"Yep! And it worked!"

Taffie was the last woman to come through the line. She reached her arms up to encircle Trista's neck. Trista whispered in her ear as they hugged, "Our prayers have been answered, Taffie. I didn't think it was ever going to happen. God is good."

Taffie nodded her head as she hugged Guss. "Welcome to the family of God, Guss. I love you."

Trista looked at the two people she loved most in the world. Life would never get any better than this, but she also knew that God had lots in store for them. They had been reading Jeremiah in their Bible study. In the book was a verse that Trista had been mulling over in her head, "For I know the plans I have for you," says the Lord. "They are plans for good and not for disaster, to give you a future and a hope. In those days when you pray, I will listen. If you look for me wholeheartedly, you will find me. I will be found by you," says the Lord.

Trista didn't understand what all that meant, but she had learned enough about God to know that as he wanted her to know, she would understand. That was good enough for her.

Life settled down into a daily routine as Taffie and Trista grew closer. Taffie wasn't as depressed, especially with the coming of spring. There was something about the budding of the flowers and the warmth of the sun that lifted her spirits and healed her heart. She still thought of Hope, but she no longer worried about dark clouds and the gloom that she felt in the days following her death.

In early May, the friends were studying a particularly difficult story in the Bible. The leader asked the women to rate the priorities in their lives. The categories were God, work, and family. Trista was struggling because she had only been half paying attention to the lessons. When it came her time to speak, she hung her head. "Well, if you want me to be honest, work is first for me. I have to work because we have to live. If I don't work, who will take care of us? Second is family. Guss is everything to me. I can't imagine life without him. Now that he has accepted Jesus, I don't have to worry about anything! As for God … well, God gets what's left. It isn't much, but he understands and loves me anyway. Doesn't he?"

The women nodded their heads in agreement. Taffie however, sat with a frown on her face. "Trista, don't you want more? What will it take for you to live for God?"

Trista looked at her friend and nodded but couldn't say anything. She had no words to say.

That night when she went home, Guss was sitting in his recliner watching TV. It wasn't anything new, but then he said, "Trista, I don't feel good. Would you feel my forehead?"

Trista felt his forehead. "You have a fever, Guss. You probably have the flu. Sleep in the chair so I don't get sick. I'll check on you in the morning. If you aren't better, you need to call the doctor." Guss nodded and pulled his blanket around his chin.

At four in the morning, Guss woke Trista. "I can't quit shaking, Trista. Can you help me?"

Trista took his temperature and found it to be 104. "Guss, you are burning up! You need to call the doctor!" Trista cried. Guss agreed to call the first thing in the morning and returned to his chair.

In the morning, Guss called the doctor. "I have a high fever and am sick to my stomach," he explained.

The doctor replied, "You probably have the flu. It's going around right now. Drink plenty of fluids and rest. If you aren't better in the morning, go to the emergency room." Guss hung up the phone, relieved that the doctor wasn't concerned.

"How are you feeling, Guss?" she asked.

"I feel a little better, Trista. I spoke with the doctor, and he said not to worry. It's probably just a bug. I'm a little hungry. Do we have any soup?"

Trista was glad that he was feeling better and hurried around the kitchen to fix his dinner. After she cleaned up the kitchen, she walked back to the living room. As she passed by Guss's chair, she looked down to see that his leg was extremely swollen and bright red. She touched it and found it to be hot as well. "Guss, what is wrong with your leg?"

Guss looked at his leg and said, "There's nothing wrong with my leg. It's just a little swollen. I think it's just because I've been lying around all day. Seriously, Trista, you worry about everything. The doctor said I was fine, remember?"

"Please, Guss, let's go to the hospital and have them check it out."

"Nothing's wrong, Trista. Please don't worry." Guss dismissed her concern again. "If it isn't better by morning, I'll call the doctor again." Trista didn't sleep that night as she worried about Guss. She prayed for God to help, but as usual, she didn't listen for a reply. All night long she tossed and turned.

Just before dawn, she finally fell into a fitful sleep. In her dreams, she saw herself before a throne. On the throne was a man, but she couldn't see his face. The light that shone into her eyes blinded her, so she kept her eyes down. She felt comforted by the presence, even though she couldn't see who was there. As she approached, she heard his voice. "Trista, come here. Let me hold you and talk to you for a bit." Trista stopped just short of the pedestal on which the throne sat.

"Are you God?" Trista asked hesitantly. "If you are, what's up with Guss? I thought you said you wouldn't ever leave us. He's sick. Can't you heal him so we can get on with our lives?" Trista just kept talking. "I don't understand. We go to church. We give money. We go to Sunday school. We're good people. Why are we going through this?" Trista waited for an answer, but just as she heard God start to speak, she heard Guss call from the living room. She sprang from the bed and ran to his side.

"Guss? What's wrong?" Trista looked at his leg with a growing fear. It was redder than the night before. She felt his forehead. He was burning with fever. "Guss, we have to go to the hospital. Get ready, and please don't argue with me." Guss nodded.

At the hospital, the doctors took one look at Guss's leg and agreed that he needed to be admitted and put on antibiotics. As he lay on the bed listening to the doctors, Trista felt her heart pounding in her chest. When the room was clear, Trista said, "Guss, I left the windows open, and I think it's going to rain. There's laundry to do, and I need to pack some clothes for you. I'll be back in a little bit.

Is there anything you need from home?" As Trista was speaking, she was backing toward the door.

Guss shook his head. "Okay, then. I'll be back in a little bit. You should be in your room by then." With those words, Trista stepped through the door and turned toward the exit. As the exit door swished open, Trista ran through it toward her car. She was barely containing the sobs. When she got to her car, she opened the door with trembling hands. She picked up her cell phone and called Taffie. As she waited through three rings, the tears ran down her face. When the automated message came on she left a message. "Taffie, Guss is in the hospital. They're going to admit him and give him antibiotics and Taffie … " Trista's control gave way as she started sobbing. "Taffie, please call me. Please."

Trista disconnected the call and laid her head on the steering wheel as she allowed her sobs to come. Some time later she lifted her head and dried her tears. She had to get out of there. At home, she closed the windows and started some laundry. She wandered around the house picking something up here and laying it there. All the time she was muttering to herself. "I don't know what to do. Give me strength. Help me!" Finally she sat down on Guss's side of the bed. She knew she should pray, but she didn't know what to say. She felt alone and abandoned.

"God," she started. "God, I don't know why this is happening. I don't know what to do. In our study the other night, I said that my priorities were work, family, and then you. If you help Guss, I promise that I'll make you a priority. It will be Guss, you, and then work. Is it a deal, God? I really need to hear from you." Trista listened closely. Taffie said that God spoke to her all the time. All she heard was the ticking of the clock. "That's what I thought. You aren't listening at all."

Trista lowered her head to the bed as she slid the rest of the way down to the floor. She knew that she should get back to the hospital, but she was so tired. She laid her head against the bed and closed her eyes. For half an hour she slept. As she slept this time, she pictured herself back in the throne room, but this time she was on the lap of the man who sat on the throne. She felt his arms around her. The embrace was warm and comforting. The words he spoke to her were low and soft.

Trista woke with a sense of peace. She couldn't quite remember what she was dreaming, but she sensed that everything would turn out just fine. When she looked at the clock, she realized that she needed to get back to check on Guss. She finished her chores and headed back.

When she got out of the elevator, she saw one of her friends from her Sunday school class. They hugged as Janice said, "Guss is in a room. The guys from our class are helping him get settled. Why don't we sit here for a minute and talk?" Trista sank down into the closest chair as Janice took her hand. "What can I do to help you, Trista?"

Trista looked at Janice with tears in her eyes and shook her head. "Nothing, Janice. I went home and did some laundry and closed the windows, paid a few bills ... " Trista's voice trailed off as she looked down the hall toward Guss's room. Janice squeezed her hand as Trista resumed talking. "Thanks for asking, but I have it all under control. No need to worry about me." Janice nodded and sat with her as they talked about things that were going on in their lives.

Two hours later everyone had gone home. Trista sat in Guss's room on a hard chair beside his bed. Guss was sleeping as Taffie walked into the room. She touched her friend on the shoulder. Trista looked up with a tearstained face. She stood as Taffie reached out her arms and pulled Trista into them. Trista cried on Taffie's shoulder as Taffie patted her back. When her sobs subsided, Taffie inclined her head toward the door. "Let's go down the hall and sit." Trista nodded and followed her down the hall to the waiting area.

"What happened, Trista?" Taffie asked.

Trista explained, "He has an infection in his leg. They aren't sure how he got it. They'll give him antibiotics and continue to monitor him. So far the doctor hasn't been in to see him. What's taking so long, Taffie?" Trista tapped her foot impatiently.

Taffie asked Trista hesitantly, "Trista, have you prayed?"

Trista looked at Taffie defiantly. "Yes, Taffie, but God hasn't answered my prayers. Why is that? I told him that I'd make him a priority in my life if he helped Guss get better."

Taffie looked at Trista and smiled. "He heard you, Trista. Now we just have to wait for his answer. Do you want to pray again?" Trista nodded and joined hands with Taffie. Taffie prayed, "Father, we come before you now to pray for healing for Guss. He's yours now, Father. Please hold him tight. Be with the doctors and nurses as they care for him. And, Father, be with my dearest friend, Trista. She loves you and wants to listen to you. Please hold her close and help her to remember to pray for all of her needs. Amen."

Trista lifted her head, but didn't take her hands from Taffie's. "Taffie, do you think that Guss will … " Trista trailed off.

Taffie squeezed Trista's hands. "Don't think the worst. God is in charge and he loves Guss. He loves you, and so do I. When is the last time you ate by the way?"

Trista looked sheepishly at Taffie. "I think last night. Do you want to go to the cafeteria?" Trista and Taffie rose together and went to eat. They talked about the Bible study they were in and the deal Trista had made with God earlier. Taffie wanted to talk to Trista more about this, but Trista was eager to get back to Guss.

"Trista, call me if you need anything. I'll be by in the morning. Are you coming to church?"

Taffie paused at the door of the hospital. "Yes, I'll be there, Taffie. See you in the morning." Trista turned toward the elevators and pushed the button. As she waited for the elevator, she thought of Taffie and smiled. She was a great friend. Trista didn't know what she would have done without her friendship over the past year.

The only noise in Guss's room was the hum of the air conditioner. As Trista sat by Guss's bed, she thought about the Bible study topic again. Work, family, God. For sure she would try to be better about putting God first, but for now she had to concentrate on Guss and getting him well so that he could go home.

In the service the next morning, Trista could hardly concentrate. After the last hymn was sung, she slipped out a side door and went back to the hospital. There, she was met by one of the doctors. "Guss's kidneys aren't working. We aren't sure why, but we'll continue to watch him and decide what we should do." The doctor was kind, but he spoke quickly. Before Trista could think about any questions to ask, he was gone. She sat heavily on the chair beside the bed and took Guss's hand. As tears once again slipped down her face, she bowed her head.

"God, I need to know if you hear me. I keep asking, but you don't answer. Guss is sick and I'm afraid. Please send someone to help..." As she finished her prayer, she felt a hand on her shoulder. It was Taffie. She pulled up a chair and sat silently beside Trista. For the rest of the afternoon as hospital personnel came and went, they sat silently. Each was lost in her own thoughts. Trista was reviewing what she would have to do until Guss got home and Taffie was speaking to God.

"Father," Taffie began, "I walked this path with baby Hope a few months ago. I hate hospitals. I hate the smell and the sounds. I hate the hopeless look that is on so many faces. Can't you please heal Guss so that we can all get out of here? My precious Trista looks so tired. God, I know you're there. I remember how I felt your presence in those dark hours when I couldn't see through the clouds. Help us see your plan."

Trista lifted her head. It was getting dark. "Taffie, do you want to read a little from the

Bible?" Trista reached for the new Bible Guss had received when he was baptized.

"What do you want to hear, Trista?"

Taffie opened the book. "How about some Psalms, Taffie?"

Taffie nodded. She started with one that was familiar. Psalm 23. When she got to the part about God leading David beside the still waters, Trista put her hand on Taffie's arm and said, "He's with me, Taffie. I just have to believe that He is with me in the good times and the bad and that he's with Guss as well."

Taffie nodded. "Yes, Trista. Always. Even unto the ends of the earth."

For the next hour Taffie and Trista read from the Bible. When Taffie left, she hugged Trista. "Are you going to work tomorrow?"

Trista nodded. "Yes, they can't do without me, Taffie. I'll come here early in the morning and then again after work."

Taffie shook her head. She remembered Trista's promise to change her priorities, but knew it wasn't the time to remind her friend.

Three weeks went by as Guss remained in the hospital. It seemed like one day he was worse and then the next day he would rally. Trista read her Bible every day and prayed to God. The people of the church where she belonged stopped by to offer her encouragement. Trista was grateful for their visits. As she prayed to God to thank him for her friends, she knew that he was pleased with the outpouring of love she and Guss received. While he still wasn't any better, Trista was beginning to believe that everything really was going to be all right.

At the end of the third week Trista called Taffie in the middle of the night. In a panicked voice she said, "Taffie, the hospital just called and said that I need to come to Guss's room right away. Can you come?"

Taffie dressed and met Trista in the ICU of the hospital. Guss was having problems with his heart, but by the time Taffie reached Trista, Guss was out of danger. Taffie sat with Trista for an hour before she went home. The next day she was to take her daughter to the airport. She explained to Trista, "I won't be here, but if you need me, just call. I'll make sure that I have my phone on."

When Trista woke up on the ICU waiting room sofa, she stretched. She went into the room to see how Guss was doing. He was still on the bed as a machine did his breathing for him. The nurse was checking his IVs.

She smiled as Trista took Guss's hand. "He made it through the night, Trista. Why don't you go home and get cleaned up? Take a nap and come back in a few hours. I promise I'll call you if anything happens."

Trista nodded. There really wasn't anything she could do.

At home, she showered and laid on the bed. She closed her eyes and pulled the covers around her chin. Her hand snaked to Guss's side of the bed, but she quickly pulled it back. He wasn't there. She wondered if he would ever come back again. She willed her mind to turn off, but the thoughts of what might happen kept coming. Trista rose and sat on at the side of the bed. She thought about praying but decided that what she needed was to take a walk. She hadn't been outside since Guss went into the hospital. It was a beautiful early summer day, so she went to the park down the road.

She picked a well-worn path by the river to walk. As she walked, she sang songs softly. Her eyes focused on the path as she moved through the forest. When she came to a clearing by the river, she sat on a rock. She sat in silence for some time and then spoke. "God, I know you're there. I've heard you so many times over the past three weeks. Father God, Guss is sick. He no longer hears me when I read to him. He can't talk or even hold my hand. There are tubes everywhere and needles and machines to breathe for him…" Trista broke off as she started to cry. "Father, I'm afraid! I can't live without him. He's my life! He's the first person who loved me just as I am. Who's going to love me like that if you take him from me?" Trista bowed her head and fell to her knees. "Abba, Guss belongs to you, not to me. Jesus prayed, 'My Father, if it's possible take this cup from me. Yet I pray your will – not mine.' I pray the same, Father God. Please take this terrible time from me, and yet, whatever you say, I'll do."

When Trista said her final "amen," she stood. Somehow the fear in her heart had been replaced by a peace that she couldn't quite understand. She walked by the river until she reached the end of the path. As she backtracked, she noticed the beauty of the trees in bloom and the ducks swimming on the river. In the clearing she saw kids splashing in the water and calling to one another. As Trista walked, she continued to talk to God, and she listened to the words he spoke to her heart. She pictured God walking beside her and was comforted.

Trista got in her car and went back to the hospital. Once there she found Taffie. She looked in surprise and said, "I thought you were going to the airport today! It's good to see you, but why are you here?"

Taffie nodded. "I took Shelly to the airport and was going home, but I started praying for you, and somehow God said that I needed to come to see you. Are you doing okay?"

Trista smiled and hugged Taffie. "Yes, for the first time in three weeks I'm at peace. I walked by the river and prayed. God told me that everything was going to be fine and that I needed to trust him. He reminded me of the verse I told Guss this morning: not to worry about tomorrow, because today has troubles of its own. Taffie, what do you think that means? Do you have your Bible with you?"

Trista no more spoke those words before a voice came over the intercom asking for Trista to come to ICU. The women rose and rushed to the doors of the unit. At the entrance to Guss's room, there was a doctor waiting. Trista stopped short and looked at him. Her head felt light, and it seemed like it was getting dark, as if storm clouds were gathering.

The doctor stepped up, introduced himself, and said, "Trista, I'm so sorry, but Guss's heart stopped. We started it up again, but it was stopped too long. We have him on a respirator, but he has no brain function. We can keep him alive, but…"

Trista turned to Taffie with a puzzled look. Taffie reached out and put her arm around her friend. Trista spoke softly. "Taffie, he said everything would be okay. What? How? Taffie…" Trista couldn't think anymore. Suddenly the priority list from her Bible study came to mind. Work, Guss, God. The choice had been made for her. It was now work and God. She hadn't worked for three weeks, so that meant that only God was left.

Trista tried to process what had happened. Guss was her knight in shining armor. She sat on the floor outside his room and bowed her head. She tried to pull the vision of herself on God's lap to mind. But all she could see was darkness. She spoke as if he was there. "Where did you take him, God? Please let him come

back to me. We talked about this, and you said not to worry. Where is he?" The storm clouds gathered around her as she heard the doctor tell Taffie, "We don't have to make the decision right now. For now the machines are keeping him alive. Talk about it and have the nurse call me when she makes her decision."

Trista held up her hand. She knew what Guss wanted, and it wasn't to be kept alive by a machine. "Are you sure he isn't ever going to be okay again?" She looked hard into the doctor's eyes.

The doctor nodded. "He'll never be able to live a normal life again. The machine is keeping him alive. His brain is dead."

Trista held up her hand again. "Please don't say anymore. He's with God now. Unplug the machine. Let him go home." The doctor nodded and said a few more words of condolence and left to get the necessary paperwork.

Taffie sat on the floor beside Trista. She pulled Trista's head to her shoulder. "I'm here,

Trista. I'm so sorry. What can I do to help?" Trista looked at her blankly. She couldn't even think, much less speak. Taffie helped her to her feet and led her back to the waiting room. Once there she called Slim to let him know what had happened. Slim said that he would call the pastors of the church and a few friends.

As they sat together in silence in the empty waiting room, Taffie called out to God, "Oh, God, my Trista's lost the love of her life. Help me comfort her! I don't know the words to say to help her. I remember how lost I was in the moments after Hope died, but I can't remember what helped me!" Taffie looked at Trista and remembered the clouds that gathered around her as she lost her grandbaby. She was sad to see the same clouds now surrounding her friend.

The next few days reminded Taffie of the days after Hope's death. She and Slim tried to help Trista as much as possible, but it seemed like she had put a wall up and didn't need any help. She always had people around her, but she didn't talk much. Taffie was worried about her, but she knew that until Trista was ready there wasn't anything she could do.

The day of Guss's funeral came as family and friends came to celebrate Guss's life. Trista didn't feel much like celebrating, even though she knew that Guss and God were together now. She was lonely and angry with God. As a matter of fact, she hadn't prayed since that morning when she walked along the river. There wasn't any need. She didn't believe that he even cared, much less trust him. She knew that it wasn't the way she was supposed to think, but it was exactly what she was thinking.

As the pastors spoke the final words at the gravesite, Trista watched with dry eyes. Taffie sat beside her watching. Trista had withdrawn from all of them, and Taffie didn't know what to do. As she reached out to Trista, she prayed, but she didn't get any response from either God or Trista.

Two days later Trista scheduled an appointment with Guss's doctor. She was angry because he hadn't done anything to save Guss's life. She pretended to be sweet and kind, but deep in her eyes, dark clouds of anger were building. "Trista, let's do a thorough checkup to see where we need to work. Let's start with a mammogram," the doctor suggested. Trista didn't want to do anything the doctor told her, but after a brief argument, she agreed.

At the hospital where Guss had died less than a week before, she had a mammogram. Three weeks later when she went to the mailbox, there was a letter from the hospital. "Please come back for a follow up test. We located a suspicious place on the test result. Please schedule a follow-up as quickly as possible." Trista read the letter three more times before she laid it on the counter. It was Saturday, and she wouldn't be able to call until Monday. She picked up the phone and dialed Taffie's number.

"Taffie, I got my test results back. There's something wrong, and I have to go back for more tests. Taffie, what do you think?" Trista was worried, and didn't know what to do.

"Trista," Taffie said. "Do you want me to go with you?"

"No, Taffie, you have to work. I'll go by myself and call you when I get out." Trista wouldn't accept help from anyone. She had decided that it was too much trouble and that she could do most everything on her own. After all, God had said he would take care of everything, and he didn't do what he said he would, so why should she trust anyone?

Taffie didn't say anything on the other end of the phone. Finally Trista broke the silence. "It'll be okay, Taffie. I'll see you tomorrow in church." Sunday came and went. The women spoke for a brief time but didn't mention the upcoming tests. Monday came, and Trista scheduled the test for later that week. When she arrived at the hospital, she tried not to remember all of the things that had happened over the weeks Guss was there. It was difficult as she was afraid of the upcoming tests and what the results would be.

In the women's health office, the nurse took another mammogram. While Trista waited, the doctor looked at the pictures and decided that she would need to go to another part of the hospital for further tests. They next did an ultrasound sonogram. As the nurse finished, she said to Trista, "Go ahead and get dressed, but don't leave. The doctor will be in to see you."

Trista dressed and waited in the room for the doctor. As she sat on the cold, hard chair, she wished that she had asked Taffie to come with her. She really didn't want to be alone, but it was difficult to ask for help. The doctor came into the room with a new nurse. He put the pictures on the reader and started pointing to a dark area on the screen. "Trista, what we see is a mass…" Trista didn't hear anymore. She had the same buzz in her ears as she had that day in the ICU when she received the bad news that Guss was gone.

The doctor looked at the nurse and nodded. The nurse came to Trista and touched her on the shoulder. Trista jumped and looked startled. The nurse said, "Trista, did you hear what the doctor said? You have breast cancer. We don't know yet if it is malignant or not. We'll do more tests to find that out. What are you thinking?"

Trista looked at both of them with tears streaming down her face and said, "My husband died in this hospital four weeks ago. I can't do this now. What am I going to do?"

The doctor looked at her with steely eyes and said, "We can do this anywhere you want, but don't wait. You need to get this taken care of. Do you understand, Trista?"

The nurse looked at the doctor and nodded. "Can you give us a few minutes?"

The doctor turned off the lights on the screen and walked past Trista to the door. As he walked past her, he paused and squeezed her shoulder. "It's going to be okay, Trista."

After he exited, the nurse kneeled down in front of Trista as she sobbed her heart out.

Trista called Taffie when she got home. She had to leave a message. Taffie went to Trista's house as soon as she heard. The women cried together as Trista told the story. Taffie asked Trista if she wanted to pray, but Trista just shrugged. "You pray, Taffie. God listens to you. Me? Not so much." Taffie grabbed Trista's hands and prayed to God for mercy and healing for her friend. When she finished, Trista thanked Taffie for coming over and said that she'd let her know how the tests came out.

The day of the biopsy, Trista's aunt and Taffie went to the hospital with Trista. They waited for what seemed like eternity as Trista underwent the biopsy. The results were back. Cancer. Trista had cancer, and it seemed like the whole world had stopped. Trista couldn't ever remember such a dark cloud being over her. When her aunt tried to comfort her, she only stared straight ahead. When Taffie talked to her, she would speak, but it wasn't the same Trista that Taffie knew.

"Taffie, I have cancer." Trista's eyes closed as the tears poured from her eyes. "Why did God allow me to have cancer? Doesn't he love me? Doesn't he care? Taffie, I'm done with God. He hasn't spoken to me in a long time anyway. I'm tired. I think I'll go to bed now."

Trista thought about what it would be like to close her eyes and never wake up again. Would she wake up in a different place or was that all a story? Would she wake up in the arms of God or maybe even Guss? It seemed so easy and comforting to just go to sleep and never have to wake up again. Trista was drifting off to sleep when the last thought hit her.

Where did those thoughts come from? she wondered. She knew better. Taffie had reminded her just that afternoon that God had a plan for her life and that it would prosper her and not harm her. Now she was thinking about harming herself. She thought of Taffie and wondered if Taffie was praying for her in that moment. She was sure it was the case. She decided that it was time to pray as well.

"God, I'm sorry that I haven't been praying or reading my Bible. I know that you're there. Could you help we me walk through this darkness? The storms are raging all around, and I'm afraid. Could you just hold me? I'm so tired." Trista's eyes closed and she fell into a deep sleep. As she slept, she once again climbed up into the lap of God, and as she closed her eyes once again, she noticed clouds all around her with a single beam of light piercing the dark sky. She smiled and slept.

For the next thirty weeks, Trista fought cancer. Taffie was amazed at the way that Trista battled her way through the dark times, but she knew that it was power from God and not from Trista. She was glad that Trista was so strong, but she worried that her friend refused help. She continually spoke to God about the situation.

The last treatment came on Trista's birthday. It was a great day of celebration for all of them. As Taffie and Trista chatted, Taffie reminded Trista of her priority list from the year before. "Trista, do you remember when you said that your priorities were work, family and God?" Trista nodded and Taffie continued. "Has that changed?"

Trista looked at Taffie with a chagrined look on her face. "Yes, Taffie. It used to be work, family, God. When Guss died, it was God for a little while. Soon it was back to work, God. When I got sick, it was God. I think it's always been God, Taffie. He's been talking to me all along, but I don't think that I knew how to listen. I'm so glad that he never gave up on me, even when I gave up on him."

Taffie smiled and patted Trista's hand. "Me too, Trista. When Hope died I remember feeling like there was nothing but clouds all around me. I saw the same thing happen to you when all of your troubles came. I'm not sure what the clouds are all about, but I know that God will tell us when the time comes. For now, let's thank God for bringing you through

your cancer." The ladies bowed their heads and gave thanks to God for healing Trista.

That autumn, Taffie and Trista decided to go away for a long weekend to visit Trista's aunts and uncles. It was October, and all of the trees were dressed in their beautiful fall colors. As Taffie and Trista were driving through the mountains, they got lost, as they so often did when they traveled together. On the top of the mountain, they hit a heavy fog bank. Trista slowed the car to a safer speed to travel. When they came off the mountain, there was a clearing in which they could see for miles in every direction as the sun shone through.

Taffie looked at Trista with tears flowing down her cheeks. "Trista, it's just like when the clouds were over us and we couldn't see what God was doing in our lives! Do you remember when it was so dark, and then without warning, we could see that there was hope even in the tough times? It was as if we could hear God himself speaking to us through the clouds!" Trista looked at Taffie in amazement. She didn't realize that the storm clouds could be important in their walk with God.

"But what do the clouds mean, Taffie?" asked Trista.

Taffie replied, "I'm not sure, Trista, but I know that God will show us when he's ready. Do you want to sing?" Trista loved to sing, so she turned up the CD player and sped up as the women joined voices to sing "How Great Thou Art." Trista lifted one hand as she was driving. They went in and out of the fog as they continued to sing praises with tearstained faces. Soon they were on the right path again and on their way to the cabin.

When they arrived at their destination, they spent time hiking and talking as well as studying the Bible and praying. They watched as the last of the leaves on the trees rustled in the wind. Taffie reminded Trista of the verse they had read this morning in their devotion time. "Trista, Isaiah 55:12 says, 'You will go out in joy and be led forth in peace; the mountains and hills will burst into song before you, and all the trees of the field will clap their hands.' Do you want to sing with the mountains?"

The girls simultaneously started singing, "Great Is Thy Faithfulness" as they walked. The two friends knew that winter was coming, but for the moment they were content to be together.

When they got home, Trista bought a new house at the same time Taffie had a new grandbaby. Her daughter named him Gabriel. He was fat and squirmy, but more important, healthy. Taffie fell in love with him, as did Slim. Trista held him with wonder in her heart as well.

Gabriel was a gift from God. He hardly ever cried. As Taffie grew to know him in those first few weeks, she fell more in love. She thanked God for his gift. She knew that Gabriel couldn't replace Hope, but she certainly appreciated him more since she had lost so much when Hope died.

As it goes in life, spring made way to summer and summer to fall. Trista and Taffie made plans to go back to the hills. They hadn't spent much time together, as both of them were busy with their lives. Trista had returned to work, and Taffie was busy with Gabriel and Elouise. Taffie's mother-in-law wasn't feeling well, so Taffie spent a lot of time with her. Taffie and Trista spoke on the phone every night.

One night, Trista asked Taffie to come to her house to talk with her. Taffie put the handset back into the cradle and spoke to Slim, "Trista wants me to come to her house to talk. Do you suppose she's sick again?"

Slim hugged Taffie and told her to go to Trista's house. "I don't know, Taffie, but go and check it out. I'll be here when you get back."

Taffie drove to Trista's house. As she drove, she prayed for wisdom. Once inside Trista's house, Taffie got a bottle of water and sat down. "Trista, is everything all right? What's going on?"

Trista gave a short laugh. "Don't worry, Taffie! Everything's fine! I had a dream about you and me, and God I wanted to talk to you about. You were in it, so I thought I'd tell you about it. I've been praying about it all day."

Taffie drew a deep breath. A dream. "Tell me, Trista," she said as she sat back in her chair.

Trista drew her feet under her as she started. "I went to the throne room. Do you remember me telling you about those dreams before?" Taffie nodded. Trista continued. "This time you were with me. We kneeled before the throne and asked God if we could talk to him. He held out a scepter and asked us to come forward. I asked him, 'God, I know that you've called Taffie and me to work for you, but we aren't sure what we're supposed to do. When I accepted you as my Lord, you said that nothing would ever happen again. God, my life has been as dark as night—so dark I couldn't even see an inch in front of my face. Were you there the whole time? What were you thinking? I almost stopped believing. I need to understand, Father.

How can I help others understand when I don't understand myself?'"

At that point, you replied, "Trista, could you stop talking for a minute and let God talk to you?"

"What did God say then, Trista?" Taffie laughed. She could picture Trista with her hands on her hips, lecturing God.

"Well, Taffie," Trista retorted, "he told you to stop scolding me. He said he was used to me and the way that I never stop talking." Trista stopped and looked at Taffie as she was smirking. "Taffie … "

"I'm sorry, Trista. Continue with your dream."

Trista continued. "God said to me, 'Trista, you're prideful. I'm working on you to burn that out of you. Do you think that you would be the same person if you hadn't gone through these storms with the dark clouds?'"

"I looked pensively at God. 'I suppose not. I guess that I couldn't appreciate the beam of light if I hadn't lived in the dark. Can I ask another question?' God nodded. 'Why one storm right after another? Why couldn't you cut me some slack?'"

"God looked at me for a full minute before he answered. 'Trista, my Word says that the light and power that shine in you is held in a perishable container, that is, in your weak body. So everyone can see that your glorious power is from me and not your own. The Bible says that you are pressed on every side by troubles but not crushed and broken. You are perplexed, but you don't give up and quit. You are hunted down, but I never abandoned you. You get knocked down, but you get up and keep going. Your job now is to go to the neighborhood and spread the word of how I worked in your life. Does that help you, Trista?'"

"Then what happened, Trista?" Taffie asked.

Trista replied, "I thought about it and then said, 'I think I do, God.' Then I asked you if you had any questions."

"What did I say?" Taffie was on the edge of her seat now.

"Well, you asked God what it was that you were supposed to be doing. You said you were confused."

Taffie leaned forward. "What did he say?"

"He said, 'Taffie, I'll show you when I'm ready. Until then, keep studying and praying. There'll be a time when I'm going to use all of the hurts and joys and trials and clouds to bring comfort to others. Be ready!'"

Taffie clapped her hands. "Trista, that's wonderful. What happened next?"

Trista said, "We left the throne room, and then I woke up."

Taffie sighed. "I would have loved to see what the end of the story was, Trista. Let me know if you dream it again."

Trista nodded and rose. "Do you want to go for a walk, Taffie?"

Taffie jumped up and started for the door. As the women walked down the sidewalk, they joined hands like schoolgirls. They talked and walked for over an hour as they tried to decide what God would do with their lives.

The sun was going down as Trista asked Taffie, "Taffie, do you want to go visit Gabriel? How about Elouise? What's she doing tonight? What do you want to do? Would Slim like to go with us?"

"Trista, stop!" Taffie laughed. "You're too busy. How do you ever hear God talk much less me?"

Trista grinned sheepishly as they continued to walk. "Taffie?" Trista spoke again. "Can I ask a question?"

Taffie stopped in her tracks. "Trista! You can ask one question, and that's it!"

Trista squeezed her hand and asked, "Do you know where we are?"

Taffie looked exasperated. "I thought you knew! Oh, Trista we're lost again!"

Trista looked at the streets in front of her and said, "I don't think we're lost, but we need to be going toward the west, and I think we're headed east. It's getting dark. We'd better turn around so that we can get home." With that, the friends did an about face. As they turned, giggling, they stopped in their tracks and fell to their knees in unison.

"Trista, look," Taffie said softly. She looked at Trista, who was kneeling with tears running down her face. Before them was the most glorious sunset either of them had ever seen. They watched it until the sun set below the horizon and then rose and started for home. Taffie was the one to break the silence. "Trista, what do you think the clouds mean?"

Trista put her arm around Taffie as they continued to walk. "I think each of the clouds are the difficult times we have in life, Taffie. Remember the clouds we saw tonight? There were two gold ones over there. Maybe they were the two babies you gave away. And do you remember the heart-shaped one to the north?" Taffie nodded. "Maybe that one was your baby Hope who died. And the blustery one? I think we'll call that one Guss! There were clouds of every color, size, and shape. Even the black clouds that would seem so ominous all alone in the sky weren't so scary with the white puffy clouds breaking up the scene. What do you think, Taffie?"

Taffie was still for a moment as she thanked God for Trista. When she spoke she said, "Trista, I think the clouds are all about the glory of God showing through in every situation in our lives. No matter what he uses every cloud to show us his majesty. I think we need to sing."

So the girls linked arms and sang to God:

Praise God from whom all blessings flow
Praise him all creatures here below
Praise him above ye heavenly host
Praise Father, Son, and Holy Ghost
Amen.

Trista imagined God looking down from heaven and smiling at the two of them. She knew that there was so much to come, but that they would have to wait for God to unveil the plan. She was content with that for the time being…

. . . .

Over the next six years, the women became closer than any two sisters. Trista started teaching the ladies Sunday school class, and Taffie had many tasks serving the elderly and needy. Both of them enjoyed their lives, but eventually, as always happened, Trista became discontent. It seemed like God was trying to tell her something, but she just couldn't catch what it was he was trying to tell her. She talked about it in her class as well as to many of her friends. Taffie was the one to bear the brunt of her tirade.

One sunny Sunday morning Trista sat in the pew of her church. She sighed. Once again, God had spoken to her through the messages that morning. *God,* Trista complained inwardly, *Why do I have to teach lessons like this? Why do I have to hear the same message from the pastor that I just taught in Sunday school? Why do we have to talk about it in Bible study tonight too? Why? Why? Why?* Trista sighed again. The answers wouldn't come. God wasn't talking today she decided. It seemed like that was happening a lot again lately.

....

After the service, Trista sat at the restaurant table with Taffie and tried to complain to her. "Taffie, I just don't understand God. I taught the lesson this morning on obedience. I think that some of you must be out of God's will on something. I know that in the past I've been disobedient and have had to work on his will for my life. I've surrendered all that I can and constantly search my heart for areas where I'm out of his will for me. So it can't be my problem. Who do you think isn't hearing the message? I'd like to go to her and talk to her so that God can get on with a new topic for us."

Taffie listened with love to Trista. Trista liked to try to fix people. Taffie knew that this was a problem that Trista didn't always see in herself, but she also knew that God had been working in Trista's life through the things she'd been through over the past six years. It was amazing to see how much she'd grown in her faith. She also knew her friend well enough to know that any words she might say to Trista would be met with resistance. Sometimes it was just better to let her talk. And talk she did. No one said more words than her dearest friend Trista.

As for Taffie, the message on obedience was working in her own heart. She and God had been talking about it for some weeks. She too had areas in her life that weren't given over to God, but that was for her and God to work out, not Trista. For now, she needed to speak to Trista about the issue at hand.

"Trista, what if God's speaking to all of us? What if he wants all of us to search our hearts for areas of disobedience? Are you obedient in every area of your life? I know that I'm not, so I'm grateful for the lessons that he's teaching me." Taffie broke off her sentence and looked at Trista, who was frowning.

"Taffie, I can't think of anything that I'm not one hundred percent obedient in right now," Trista said defiantly. "I think that it's someone else."

Taffie wisely kept her mouth shut, sensing that Trista was battling another pride issue. "Okay, Trista. Time will tell. Let's go see Elouise. She's lonely and will be glad to see us."

Trista nodded and gathered her things. Elouise She now lived in the nursing home, as her health was failing. Trista also knew that Elouise was in a place with people who loved her and would care for her better than anywhere else. She loved to see Elouise and talk to her. The older woman had wisdom to share, and Trista was like a sponge, soaking up the wisdom and stories that she told.

Taffie and Trista spent several hours sitting in the sun with Elouise in the courtyard of the nursing home. When the time came for them to leave, Taffie pushed Elouise back to her room in the wheelchair. Trista bent over and hugged the thin frame of the woman she loved.

"I love you, Elouise," she whispered.

"I love you too, Trista," Elouise replied in a wavering voice. "Come back soon."

"See you at choir practice, Taffie." With those words, Trista's mind was off to the next place she needed to be.

Trista was always racing here and there. She knew that God knew how she was and that he would always be there to talk to her when she needed him. She often daydreamed entire conversations as she was driving to her meetings or to the store. She loved those times. Today was no different, but she was still focused on the problem in church. If she could just put her finger on it …

The problem was that when Trista got into her car, she opened the windows and turned up the CD for the Christmas musical they were singing at church. She couldn't hear God, even if he did speak, as the music blared in the speakers.

Trista ran a stop sign on the street where she was to pick up her friend, Melissa.

"Hi, Missy! Are you ready for choir practice tonight?" Missy hopped into the car and started talking a mile a minute about the things going on in her life. Before long, they were at the church where they worshiped. They sat through choir practice and then went to Bible study, where they were doing a particularly difficult topic.

Patsy, the Bible study leader, was leading them in a study of prayer. It was difficult for Trista, as she didn't have enough time to devote to the study and still do the other work she was doing for God. It was a never-ending problem for her, and one that they discussed at length that night. When they finished, Trista and her friends parted with hugs. Missy chattered all the way home. When Trista dropped her off, suddenly the evening seemed to be too quiet. She reached for the radio, but in the instant before she turned it on, she heard her name being called. She decided that she should pray, as it had been over a week since she'd talked to

God. She drove on instinct as she daydreamed about approaching the throne to talk to God.

"God? Is that you? I'm here!" Trista listened for what God had to say to her. She smiled to herself as she pictured herself climbing onto the lap of God. She wondered why she'd waited so long to be with him.

"Trista, I've been waiting for you for weeks. I see that you've been busy. Tell me about your life." God sat back on his throne and listened to Trista list the things that she had been doing. When she finally paused for a breath, he broke in.

"Trista, there are a few problem areas in your life that we need to talk about. Are you prepared to discuss them with me?" God looked at her, already knowing the answer.

"Not now, King, but soon. Right now I have three days of my women of fragrance study on the will of God, and my Sunday school lesson for next week to do, and I have to make time to pray, according to what Patsy told us to do tonight." She continued, "I have laundry to do and grass to cut. The car needs an oil change, and I have to clean the house for when the girls come over Thursday. Our fall drama presentation is next week, and I'm a counselor … Oh, I forgot! The D'way kids from church are coming over tomorrow to pick up the sticks and stones in the yard. I wonder if their dad will fix my siding for me? God, there is too much to do. I really don't have time to talk right now. God? God?"

Trista listened, but God was nowhere to be found. It was nothing new. It seemed like every time she spoke to him anymore, he'd listen for a while and then disappear. It hurt her feelings, but well, he was God, and he could do what he wanted. She got ready for bed and thought again of the lessons of the morning. She thought of the message of obedience and, once again, decided to pray. "God, I think I'm obedient in all areas of my life, but if not, will you show me? Once again, I'm waiting!"

She turned off the light and closed her eyes. Sleep didn't come easy lately. Tonight was no different. She tossed and turned, hitting her pillow and alternately turning on the TV and turning it off.

Finally, she fell into a fitful sleep in which she dreamed of a breakfast banquet. In the dream, she ran up and down the tables laden with food. Every dish she picked up held an unappetizing mess of green food. Each time, she would shake her head and put it back down. Up and down the tables she went all night, rejecting each plate. When she woke in the morning, the dream was still running in her head. What did it mean? By the time she was racing down the freeway to work, the dream had faded. At the last second before she walked into the door of the office, she remembered that she hadn't prayed yet.

"Father God, good morning. I love you and want your will to be done in my life today. Bless me and everyone else I talk to today.

Thank you for your blessings. Amen." With that, Trista began her day.

. . . .

That afternoon, the D'way kids went over to Trista's house. Their mom, Sha, and Trista were friends from Bible study. As she dropped the kids off, Sha hugged Trista. "Do you have a minute to sit and talk, Sha?" Trista pulled her toward the patio chairs. "I wanted to thank you for allowing the kids to come over and help me. I have such a hard time getting everything done now that Guss is gone."

Sha nodded and picked up her hand. "The kids love to help you, Trista. If you need anything, you know that you only have to ask. Right now, I have to go. Are you okay with watching them until we get home tonight?"

Trista smiled and nodded. "Leave them with me. We'll have a great time. Have fun!" The friends hugged, and Trista turned to watch the kids work.

Rhett was working hard as the other three kids lagged behind. For over an hour they picked up sticks from the windstorm on Sunday. When they were done, Trista had cookies and hot chocolate on the patio for them. She thanked each child and gave them a cookie. "Thank you, my D'way friends! You've done a great job. Your mama and papa won't be here for a while, though. What do you want to do?"

Brennan jumped up in front of Trista and yelled, "Read us a story!" The other three quickly agreed.

Trista nodded. It was their favorite thing. It was hers too. They were very smart children and a joy to be with. "What story shall we read?" Four different answers came from the four children.

"*Tommy the Train*!"
"*Horton Hears a Who*!"
"*One Fish Two Fish*!"
"*Green Eggs and Ham*!"

Trista laughed. "I can't read all of them, but how about *Green Eggs and Ham*?"

Rhett shouted, "Yeah! That's my favorite!" He raced to Trista's room to get the book. He and his brother, Brennan, settled in at Trista's feet as the two little girls cuddled up, one on each side. The older of the two girls, the one they called Cutie, shouted that she was going to turn the pages. The littlest one, Rayray, started crying. Trista pulled her close and winked at her. "Don't cry, Rayray. You can help." With that, Trista began to read.

I am Sam
Sam I am
That Sam-I-am!
I do not like
That Sam-I-am!

Trista read the words to the children, but her mind had drifted away. She found herself daydreaming again in front of the throne as she spoke to God. She'd not even thought of him all day. "Hello, God. I'm sorry that I haven't spoken with you today. I wanted to talk to you more about the lessons on Sunday morning. I think we have a problem in church. I think that some people aren't being obedient to you. I need to tell them, but I don't know who they are…"

Cutie interrupted her thoughts. "Missa Tissa, you didn't wead that page wight," she said in her little girl voice. "It says, 'I do not like gween eggs and ham.' Wead it again!" The boys on the floor nodded in agreement, so Trista turned her mind once again to the book.

"God, what do you say?" Trista settled her thoughts back on the throne as the story droned on.

God spoke, "Well, Trista, since you asked, I think it is *you* who has the problem. You say that you have surrendered your entire life over to me, but is that true? I see areas of your life that you've said are none of my business. I see that as a problem. How about you?"

"Not surrendered? No way!" Trista was instantly defensive. "You have control of my entire life! I can't think of one thing that you could want me to do that I wouldn't say 'yes' to immediately."

"How about your personal life, Trista?" God always got right to the point. "Would you ever date a man?" Trista's ears started to burn. He was treading on a subject that was not open for discussion.

"I would not care to date a man. I would not like that, God-I-AM." In the background, Trista heard howls of laughter. She turned her attention back to the children. "What's so funny?" Rhett and Brennan were rolling about on the floor, laughing.

"You said, 'I would not care to date a man,' not 'I do not like green eggs and ham!' Miss Trista, you made a funny!"

Trista glared at the unruly boys. "Boys, quit, or else we will put the book away. Now let's get back to the story."

I would not eat green eggs and ham
I do not like them, Sam-I-am.
Would you? Could you?
In a car? Date him! Date him!
If he were a star?
I would not, could not, in a car.
I would not, would not, date a star!
I would not care to date a man
I would not like that, God-I-AM.
A brain! A brain!
A brilliant brain
Could you, would you, if he had a brain?
Not with a brain,
Not on a train!
Just the thought would cause great pain!
Not in a car! Nor date a star!
Please hear my plea
And leave me be!
I will not date one here or there.
I will not date one anywhere.
I do not want to date a man.
I do not want to, God-I-AM!
Say! In the park? Here in the park!
Would you, could you, in the park?

Back and forth God and Trista went as she shot down every scenario that he put forth. Meanwhile, the children were laughing hysterically at Trista, but she no longer heard them. She was too busy arguing with God.

Could you, would you, with an old goat?
Would you, could you, if he had a boat?
I could not, would not, even if he could float!
I will not date him with a brain.
It would give me quite a pain!
Not in a car! Nor date a star!
I would not date a total fox.
You must, you must, be off your blocks!
I would not date him in my house.
What if he's a total louse?
Would you give him half a chance?
You joke! You joke!
What if he's broke?
I know you think I'm full of pride!
But I couldn't because …

At this, Trista paused and then continued with a loud shout.

What if his hair he dyed?
I would not date one here or there!
I would not date one anywhere!
I don't have time to date a man!
I work for you, great God-I-AM![1]

Trista's ears were buzzing. She realized that she was standing in the middle of the living room with her hands clenched at her sides. Cutie and Rayray were on the floor beside the sofa. When she jumped up off the sofa, she had thrown them to the ground. Brennan was on all fours with a pillow over his head, and Rhett was sitting on the floor with a single tear running down his face.

Cutie was the first one to speak. "Miss Tissa, Mama says that we have to 'spect God, but you yelled at him. Are you mad at God?"

Rayray spoke next. "Missa Tissa, Mama gives us time-out when we awe bad. Do you need a time-out?"

The boys sat in silence as Trista sat slowly on the sofa. She pulled the little girls to her

sides. "Miss Trista is not behaving very well. Maybe I do need a time-out. How about if I take you home and we get ready for bed?" The children hung their heads. Trista gathered them up and took them home.

As they came in the door of the D'way house, Trista looked at the children. They looked so sad. She gave each one a hug and then asked Rhett to help the little ones get into their pajamas so that she could pray. "Miss Trista, can I tell you something?" Rhett started to explain.

"Not now, Rhett. Do as I asked."

Rhett nodded and turned down the hall. As the children left, Trista sunk to her knees. "God," she started, "please forgive me. Cutie was right. I was disrespectful to you. I'm sorry." She breathed deeply as she tried to imagine the safe place she went to pray. As always, she pictured herself in the throne room, where she imagined God lived. As she calmed her mind, she felt the presence that she longed for. In her dream, she lifted her tearstained face to see God holding his arms out to her. She ran into them and buried her head in his neck.

He held Trista as she wept. When she calmed, he took his scarred hand and wiped her tears away. He opened a bottle beside the throne and poured the tears into it. "Trista, what's wrong? Why are you holding back from me? Don't you know I love you and have a plan for your life?"

Trista nodded. "God." The tears started pouring again. "I'm afraid. I'm so afraid to date a man. I'm so afraid, great God-I-AM." He nodded wisely. These were the words he had been waiting for. "I know, Trista. Can you tell me what you're afraid of?"

Trista looked at him on his throne. "You know everything about me, God. You know when I get up and when I sit down. You know when I laugh and when I cry. You know my heart. Please don't make me say this. Isn't it enough that I have committed my life to spreading the good news of your healing hand?"

God held her tight. "Say it, Trista. The truth will set you free."

Trista looked at her king. "I'm afraid to date a man—here, there, or anywhere. When I said the line about 'what if his hair he dyed,' what I wanted to say is 'what if *he* died?' I can't hurt like that again, Father. Please don't make me. I will do anything else you ask, just not that."

At that time, the children came back into the room. Trista gave them each a snack and then tucked them into their beds. "Sleep tight, my D'way children. I love you, and so does God. Say your prayers and go to sleep."

She quietly shut their doors and went back to the living room to pray again. A few minutes later, a door squeaked open, and Rhett came into the room. "Miss Trista?"

Trista looked at him and smiled. "Rhett, you're supposed to be in bed. What is it?"

Rhett started to cry. Trista gathered him into her arms and hugged him tight. "What's wrong, Rhett? Are you still upset that I yelled at God? He and I have been talking, and he has forgiven me. Will you forgive me?"

Rhett looked and her and nodded his head. "You need to forgive me, Miss Trista. I asked God to send you a new husband!"

Trista looked at Rhett with a puzzled expression. "Why would you ask God for a new husband for me, Rhett?"

"Well, Miss Trista, your house is too quiet. You don't have anyone to pick up your sticks and stones, and you have that really neat tractor in your garage. You need a husband to help you! So I asked God to send you one, but when you read the story, you said you didn't want one, so …"

Rhett hung his head. Trista lifted his chin and set a kiss on his forehead. "Thanks, Rhett, for wanting more for me than I wanted for myself. You're a kind and loving boy. I love you!" She hugged him one last time and took him back to bed. When she tucked him in, she touched his hair and spoke softly. "Thanks, God, for this precious child. Thanks for speaking through him to my heart tonight. Help me to understand your will for my life through the heart of a child. Amen."

Trista returned to the living room once again. It had been an emotional night. It was the anniversary of her wedding to Guss, and the memories made her sad.

"God, is Guss okay? I know that he's there with you. Please tell him once more that I love him and miss him. I think that I understand the lesson of today. It isn't about dating. It's about what I tell you that I will and won't do. It's about obedience, isn't it?" God nodded from his throne and smiled at his favorite child. "Yes, Trista, it's about obedience— always and only. The person in church I have been speaking to is you. You need to remember that I know best for your life, and when you tell me 'no,' my work can't be accomplished in you and through you. This is only one small area of your life that needs to be addressed. Do you want to know the others now? The real question, Trista, is: Will you obey me in all areas of your life? Well, will you?"

Trista sighed. "Will I have to marry this man? Will I have to, God-I-AM?" The King threw back his mane of hair and roared with laughter.

"Trista, you don't have to marry the first man who asks you!" Trista looked at him darkly.

"I did both other times!" she retorted.

"So you did, Trista, so you did! I had forgotten. No, Trista, what I'm asking is for you to open your heart to a new adventure. I'm looking for a willing heart."

Trista nodded. "Okay, God. I will obey. But … God?" He looked at her. "Can you make it someone who likes Taffie? I don't want to have to lose her for some man."

He nodded. "Yes, Trista, my plans don't include separating you and Taffie. You have a lot of work to do together, and I do so love the way that the two of you play together. I loved when you sang songs to me last night. It blessed my heart!"

Trista said goodbye as she hugged him. It had been a long day. She took out her Bible and began to read. She smiled and thought of the dream of the green food on the banquet tables. *Green eggs and ham. Well, maybe, just maybe, great God-I-AM*, she thought.

. . . .

Meanwhile, Taffie was talking to her sister on the other side of town. "Marie, what's up in your life?"

Marie smiled. She hadn't spoken with Taffie for several months. "Well, Taffie, I'm glad you called. Do you remember my brother-in-law, KC?" Taffie nodded. "Didn't his wife die earlier this year?"

"Yes," Marie said. "He wants to start dating. Do you know of a Christian woman fifty to sixty years old who would like to go out with him?"

Taffie smiled. "How about Trista? I'm not sure that she's interested, but do you think I should ask her?" The sisters talked about it for another few minutes before Taffie said, "Okay, I'll see what she says and get back with you. Thanks for calling me."

Trista was at her desk working when Taffie called her. "Trista, are you busy?"

Trista sat back in her chair. She needed a break and was glad to hear Taffie's voice. They hadn't spent much time together lately. "What's up, Taffie?"

"Well," Taffie started to wonder if she should say anything to Trista. She didn't want to cause problems.

"Taffie? What's wrong?" Trista could hear the hesitation in Taffie's voice.

Taffie decided to ask. "You remember my sister, Marie?" Trista nodded as if Taffie could see her. "Well, Marie called this morning and asked if I knew of a Christian woman fifty to sixty years old who would like to date her brother-in-law. His wife died earlier this year, and I thought of you…" Taffie broke off. "Do you think that you would be interested in dating again, Trista?"

Trista felt the heat rise in her face. "Taffie, I don't know. Can I think about it?"

Trista frowned then said, "Wait. Taffie, go ahead and ask him to call me. What do you think? Oh, Taffie, I don't know! What should I do?"

Taffie waited for Trista to settle before she spoke. "Trista, I know KC. He's a good man. Why don't you give it a chance?"

Trista sighed. "Okay, Taffie. If you say he's a good guy, then I trust you."

The girls chatted for a few more minutes before they hung up. Trista looked at her computer screen but didn't see any of the details. She wondered if she was making a mistake. She had a good life, even if she wasn't married. She had friends and church and Bible study. She liked to read and cook. Why did she need to date? She picked up the telephone to call Taffie back and tell her that she'd changed her mind. Instead, she decided to pray.

"God, I'm back about this dating thing. Remember how I said that I didn't want to date ever again? Well, Taffie just called me … " Trista closed her eyes and pictured God on his throne. The next thing she knew, she was talking a mile a minute to him.

She saw God hold up a hand as she continued to complain. "Trista," he said, "will you let me talk? We've been over all of this before. I have a plan for your life. You need to learn to trust me. Take the risk, Trista. I won't let anything happen to you."

Trista looked at God and slowly nodded. She knew that God had always been there for her in the good times and bad. There really wasn't any reason not to trust him. She opened her eyes as the telephone on her desk rang. It was Taffie again.

"Trista, Marie said that KC would call you. Are you excited?"

Trista smiled. She thought about her conversations with God over the issue. "Yes, Taffie, I'm excited and scared all at the same time! When do you think he'll call?"

. . . .

Two weeks later the phone rang as Trista was fixing dinner for two of her friends. Trista answered. "Hi! This is Trista!"

The voice on the other end spoke quickly. "Hi, Trista. This is KC. Marie told me to call you. Am I calling at a bad time?"

Trista looked at her visitors and covered the mouthpiece of the phone. "It's him!" she mouthed with her eyes wide open. Her friends started laughing behind their hands as they made kissing noises. Trista quickly went onto the patio. "Trista, are you there?" he asked.

"Yes, KC, I'm here. I'm glad you called. How are you?"

"I'm fine, Trista. It's nice to talk to you too. I got your number from Taffie and Marie. My wife died in January, and I asked Marie if she knew of any women who might like to date. Well, you already knew that," KC broke off awkwardly.

Taffie quickly asked, "Where do you work?"

"I've worked at the hospital for over thirty years."

Trista pulled a mental chalkboard up and made an imaginary check mark beside a box that said "stable job." "Do you have kids, KC?"

KC said, "I have two beautiful daughters and four grandkids."

"Boys or girls?"

KC replied, "Yes."

Trista laughed and said, "Yes? Are they boys or girls?"

KC laughed back and said, "Yes, they are boys or girls. Sorry, I like to kid around. I have two grandsons and two granddaughters."

Trista pulled the mental chalkboard back up and checked the box beside "sense of humor." "What do you like to do for fun, KC?" Trista settled back in her chair on the patio as the sun was setting.

"Well, I like to ride my bike, and I have a scooter. I like movies and ..." Trista listened as KC described the last movie he went to see. When he finished, Trista asked him hesitantly, "Taffie said that your wife passed away. I'm sorry to hear that. Have you had a hard time adjusting?"

KC was quiet for a moment. "Jenn was sick for quite awhile before she died. I miss her terribly some days. Some days I can hardly remember what she looked like or sounded like. That makes me sad. How did you get on with your life after your husband died?"

Trista told him the story of how Guss died. When she finished, both of them were quiet. "KC, I don't understand how it works, but if you're just patient one day, it doesn't hurt so much. I don't think we'll ever forget Jenn or Guss, but after a few years, it doesn't make me cry the way it did the first year or two.

"Trista," KC said, "I don't know why, but I feel as though I've known you all my life. You're easy to talk to. Thanks for listening to me." Trista looked at her watch when KC said, "We've been talking for three hours, Trista! I think that's about all I can think of to talk about. Do you like to drink coffee?"

Trista nodded as they made arrangements to meet Monday morning for coffee. Trista hung up with KC and called Taffie immediately. "Taffie, guess what!" Trista practically screamed into the phone. "He called me! He wants to go for coffee! What should I wear? What will I say? Taffie, what if … "

Taffie broke in laughing. "Trista! Stop! It's just coffee. I'm excited for you though. Tell me what he said." Trista reviewed the conversation as Taffie listened in silence. She didn't hear all the details, as she was praying and thanking God for this new opportunity in Trista's life.

The conversation ended as Trista's phone gave a warning beep that it was about to die. "Taffie, I'll call you later. Thanks for having KC call me."

Monday dawned, and Trista was up early. She changed clothes three times before she settled on an outfit. She stood in front of the mirror and looked at the reflection as she sighed. She was as ready as she would ever be. As she came from the bathroom, she saw that she still had a half hour before she was to meet KC. She knelt by her bed as she decided to pray.

"God, I'm afraid. Please help me know what to say. Taffie and I have prayed for this moment for six years, but now that it's here … " Trista continued to pour her heart out to God. When she rose, she looked at the clock and realized that she only had ten minutes to get there. She raced from the house, arriving at the coffee shop right on time. When she arrived, she bought herself a cup of coffee, uncertain if she should buy her own or let him buy it. She decided to declare her independence and buy her own cup of coffee. As she carried it to the table, she rolled her eyes at herself. She was acting like a schoolgirl on a first date instead of a grown woman meeting for a simple cup of coffee.

KC entered a few minutes after she sat at the table. Trista looked at him and noticed his eyes immediately. They were a beautiful shade of blue mixed with flecks of green. He greeted her and introduced himself with a sweeping bow. Looking at her cup of coffee, he raised his eyebrow and said "I'll be right back. Can I get you anything?"

Trista shook her head as her cheeks turned pink. KC bought a cup of coffee at the counter and strolled back to the table, greeting a few people on the way back. He sat down and asked her, "Have you been here long?"

KC smiled. As Trista looked at him, she first noticed his dimples and then the kindly wrinkles around his eyes. She quickly averted her eyes. "Not long, KC. Thanks for asking me out for coffee. Did I tell you that I once wanted to own a coffee shop?" Trista chatted nervously.

KC smiled and nodded as she told of how she and Taffie met. "We met in church and have been best friends ever since. Did you ever have that happen, KC? It's like she was part of my family from the very beginning!"

When she asked KC about his family, he said, "I have five sisters and two brothers." Trista pulled out her imaginary chalkboard again. Quickly she checked off the physical features box with a smile beside the checkmark. Beside the box that she imagined said "family man," she put another check. With a start she focused back on KC, realizing that he had asked her a question. "I'm sorry, KC. What did you ask me?"

KC teased, "Did I lose your attention already, Trista? I'm going to have to brush up on my charm! I asked you if you'd like to see a movie sometime. What do you think? I'll let you pick." For almost three hours they talked and laughed as they shared their lives with one another. When they finally rose, KC asked, "So, would you like to see a movie or something?"

Trista smiled. "I'd love to, KC, but I'm leaving for the Blue Ridge mountains Saturday. Can we do it after I get back?"

KC smiled. "Sure, Trista. I'll talk to you soon." When Trista got home, she called Taffie. They agreed that it had been a great first date. As she was talking to Taffie, a called beeped in. When Trista checked her messages, she found that KC had called.

"Trista, I just wanted to let you know that I had a great time. Thanks for spending your morning with me. I'll talk to you soon."

That night KC called again. "Would you like to go for a walk in the park Friday night, Trista? We could get a cup of coffee afterward. I promise I won't keep you out too late. I know you're going to be leaving in the morning on your trip, but I just wanted to spend some time with you. What do you say?"

Trista smiled and nodded then realized that KC couldn't see her. "I'd love to! What time?" They agreed on six p.m. before they hung up.

Friday was rainy, so they went back to the coffee shop where they spent their time listening to a singer and a comedian. As they left the shop, KC asked if she'd like to go for a drive. He took her through the countryside, showing her where he grew up and where some of his family lived. They talked about lots of things, but that night, KC focused on his love for God.

"Trista, he's my whole life. I can't imagine how I would've made it through the months before my wife passed away if I didn't have Christ in my life." He poured out his heart as they shared stories of meeting with God. "Trista, I didn't even know that I needed God in my life. Before my brother died, he asked me, 'KC, would you believe in God if I came back after I died and told you how wonderful heaven was?' I told him, 'Nope. I'll never believe.' One day I looked at the way I was living my life and knew that it wasn't enough. It seemed as though I was always searching for the next high. There was never enough to fill me up."

Trista nodded and put her hand over his as KC continued. "Thirty years ago I said, 'God, I don't know if you're real, but I'm willing to learn more if you're willing to teach me.' I asked my other brother to take me to church, and there I went to the altar and found Jesus. Trista, I haven't been the same since. I've made a lot of mistakes since then with friends and

family. I wish that I could say that I was the perfect Christian, but that would be a lie. The thing is, now I don't keep looking for more. I'm content with what God gives me. Well, most of the time that is. I still have a lot to learn. I wish that I understood what God has in store for me, but for now I just ask him and trust that he's going to tell me what to do. Do you ever wonder what God's doing in your life?"

Trista looked at KC with tears in her eyes as she made one last check on her chalkboard. The board was now complete with checks. The last one read, "Loves God." She spoke softly to KC. "I wonder all the time, but I rarely stop to listen to what he's saying to me, KC. I think that God's speaking to me and that it's time that I choose to listen."

That night after she was in bed, KC left her a message asking if she would go out for coffee before she traveled to her aunt's house. "Will you meet me in the morning? I don't care what time it is, just call me. I just want to say goodbye one more time."

When Trista received the message the next morning, she called KC. "I'm ready to go. It's only five a.m. Are you sure you want—"

KC interrupted her. "I'll be there in fifteen minutes. Thanks for calling me."

When Trista arrived at the coffee shop, KC was already there with two cups of coffee in his hand. He smiled at her and jerked his head toward a table on the patio. As they settled in, KC picked up Trista's hand. "Trista, thanks for meeting me this morning. I won't keep you long. I had a good time last night. Did you enjoy yourself?"

Trista was suddenly shy and uncertain about what to say. "I had a good time, KC. It seems strange to be dating again, though. Is that wrong to say?"

KC smiled and sighed. "I think it's the perfect thing to say. I feel the same way. Finish your coffee. I want to pray with you before you leave."

That week as Trista relaxed in the mountain cabin, KC called her every night. One night as she was sitting outside under a full moon and starry sky, KC asked her, "Trista, what is your perfect man?"

Trista stared at the sky. Other than the crickets chirping, the night was still. Trista closed her eyes and said, "Perfect man? No restrictions?"

KC said, "Perfect."

Trista started slowly and thought of her imaginary chalkboard. "Well, he would be funny. He would be kind. He would be stable in his job and family. He'd have beautiful eyes and deep dimples." With that, Trista's face turned red in the dark night. "Most of all, KC, he would love the Lord and live his life for him."

KC was silent on the other end. "KC? Are you there?" KC cleared his voice. "I'm here, Trista. Wow. I think if you find that guy I'll marry him!"

Trista laughed. "How about your perfect woman, KC?"

KC said, "My list is short, Trista. I want someone who loves the Lord and will love me in return. I'd like someone to share my life with."

Trista waited for him to continue. When he didn't say anymore, Trista said, "That's it? You don't want great beauty or money? Why is my list so long and yours so short?"

KC replied, "I think it's because I've lived a lot of life with that stuff, Trista, and realized that none of it satisfied me. It's really all about love. Besides that, you're beautiful! Are you trying to tell me you aren't rich?"

Trista was grateful that the tension of the moment was broken. She looked up to realize that her aunt had locked her out of the cabin, thinking she was in her bed. She shrieked as she looked at her watch and realized that it was after midnight. "KC! I'm locked out of the house, and there are bears in the woods! I have to go!"

KC said, "Goodbye! Call me back if you need me to drive down to rescue you! By the way, how will I know where you are?" Trista laughed and disconnected the call as she pounded on the door to the cabin.

Three weeks later, KC and Trista had seen each other every night. They spent their evenings talking as they sat on the patio. Each night KC left and then would call Trista to say good night. On that Tuesday night, KC got Trista's answering machine.

"Trista, I just wanted to thank you again for tonight. Honey, if Jesus came back tonight, I would tell him that this has been the best three weeks of my life. I love you, and that's a whole lot easier to say on the telephone than it is face to face. Sleep tight."

Trista listened to the message as she was getting ready to go to bed. She played it over and over and over. He loved her. She couldn't believe it. As she lay in bed, she prayed. "Thank you, Father. I didn't know. I was afraid for nothing. I do trust you."

As her eyes drifted shut, she smiled. In her dream that night she pictured the argument she'd had with God all those weeks ago. As she danced around in front of the throne, she sang, "I do so want to love this man. Thank you, thank you, God-I-Am."

Taffie was dreaming on the other side of town. In her dream, she was walking down the lane at Trista's aunt's place in the mountains. The sun was shining, and there wasn't a cloud in the sky. The flowers were in bloom. She dreamed that she was walking the lane to the pond.

There, beside the pond were KC and Trista dressed in wedding clothes. Trista was holding a bouquet in each hand. As Taffie approached Trista, she handed her the smaller of the two. The best friends smiled at one another as they turned to the pastor who was asking, "Do you, Trista, take KC ... "

The wedding was over just as the dawn broke over Grovetucky. Trista and Taffie both woke with smiles on their faces as they reached for their telephones to call one another. They both couldn't wait to share their dreams. Now to plan for the real day!

> Trust in the Lord with all your heart; do not depend on your own understanding. Seek his will in all you do, and he will show you which path to take.
>
> —Proverbs 3:5–6 (NLT)

> "For I know the plans I have for you," says the Lord. "They are plans for good and not for disaster, to give you a future and a hope. In those days when you pray, I will listen. If you look for me wholeheartedly, you will find me. I will be found by you," says the Lord. "I will end your captivity and restore your fortunes. I will gather you out of the nations where I sent you and will bring you home again to your own land."
>
> —Jeremiah 29:11–14 (NLT)

For I hold you by your right hand—I, the Lord your God. And I say to you, "Don't be afraid. I am here to help you."

—Isaiah 41:13 (NLT)

O Lord, you have examined my heart and know everything about me. You know when I sit down or stand up. You know my thoughts even when I'm far away. You see me when I travel and when I rest at home. You know everything I do. You know what I am going to say even before I say it, Lord. You go before me and follow me. You place your hand of blessing on my head. Such knowledge is too wonderful for me, too great for me to understand!

—Psalm 139:1–6 (NLT)

You keep track of all my sorrows. You have collected all my tears in your bottle. You have recorded each one in your book.

—Psalm 56:8 (NLT)

Endnotes

1. Dr. Seuss, *Green Eggs and Ham,*
   1960 Random House